·LEWIS·CARROLL·

# THE WALRUS
## —·AND·—
# THE CARPENTER

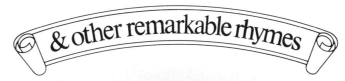

*& other remarkable rhymes*

*Illustrated by Julian Doyle*

TEMPLAR

**A TEMPLAR BOOK**

Selected and produced by The Templar Company plc
Pippbrook Mill, London Road, Dorking, Surrey RH4 1JE, England

Designed by Mick McCarthy
Printed and bound in Italy

*Back cover photo courtesy of Mary Evans Picture Library*

ISBN 1-898784-42-6

# —·CONTENTS·—

THE WALRUS AND THE CARPENTER ............... 4

A-SITTING ON A GATE ........................... 16

HOW DOTH THE LITTLE CROCODILE ............ 20

YOU ARE OLD, FATHER WILLIAM ..................... 22

THE LOBSTER QUADRILLE ...................... 28

THE GARDENER'S SONG ...................... 30

TURTLE SOUP ..................... 36

JABBERWOCKY ....................... 38

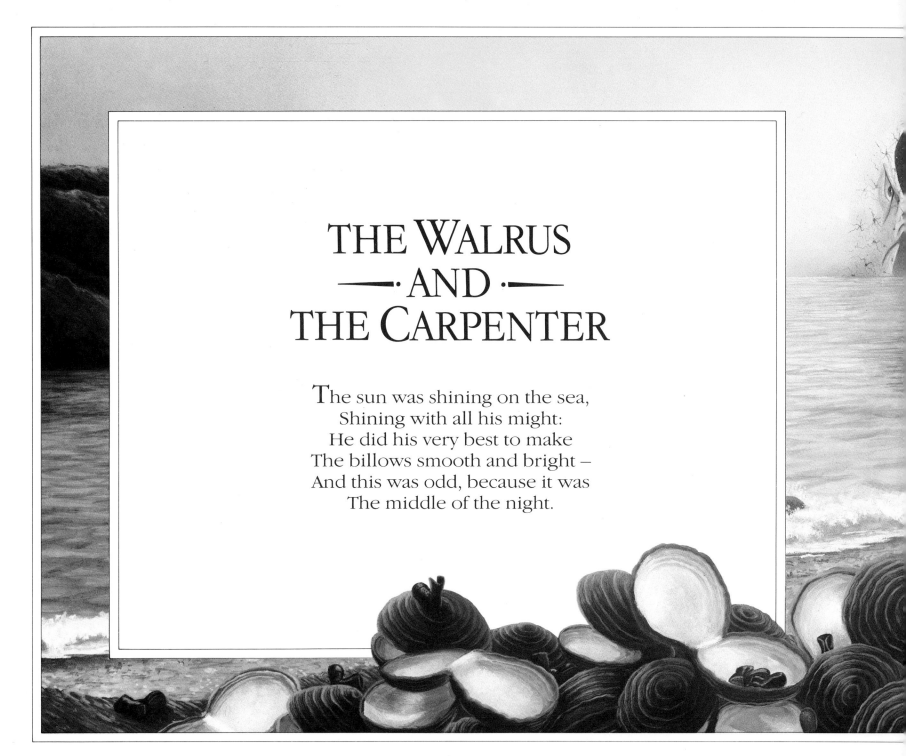

# THE WALRUS
## · AND ·
# THE CARPENTER

The sun was shining on the sea,
Shining with all his might:
He did his very best to make
The billows smooth and bright –
And this was odd, because it was
The middle of the night.

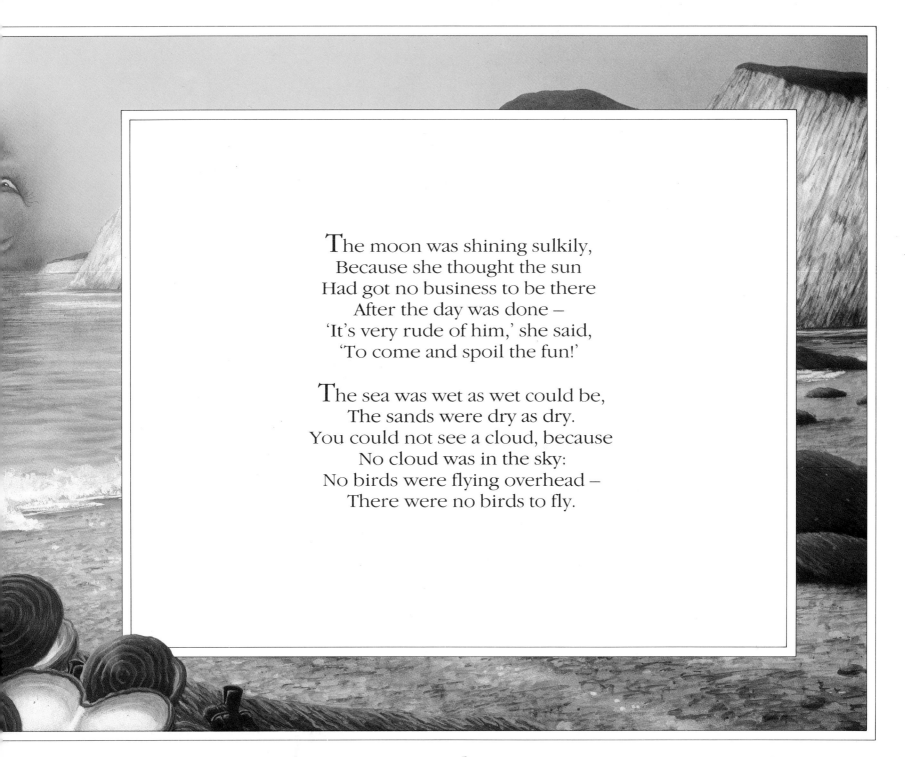

The moon was shining sulkily,
Because she thought the sun
Had got no business to be there
After the day was done –
'It's very rude of him,' she said,
'To come and spoil the fun!'

The sea was wet as wet could be,
The sands were dry as dry.
You could not see a cloud, because
No cloud was in the sky:
No birds were flying overhead –
There were no birds to fly.

The Walrus and the Carpenter
Were walking close at hand;
They wept like anything to see
Such quantities of sand:
'If this were only cleared away,'
They said, 'it *would* be grand.'

'If seven maids with seven mops
Swept it for half a year,
Do you suppose,' the Walrus said,
'That they could get it clear?'
'I doubt it,' said the Carpenter,
And shed a bitter tear.

'O Oysters, come and walk with us!'
The Walrus did beseech.
A pleasant walk, a pleasant talk,
Along the briny beach:
We cannot do with more than four,
To give a hand to each.'

The eldest Oyster looked at him,
But never a word he said:
The eldest Oyster winked his eye,
And shook his heavy head –
Meaning to say he did not choose
To leave the oyster-bed.

But four young Oysters hurried up,
All eager for the treat:
Their coats were brushed, their faces washed,
Their shoes were clean and neat –
And this was odd, because, you know,
They hadn't any feet.

Four other Oysters followed them,
And yet another four;
And thick and fast they came at last,
And more, and more, and more –
All hopping through the frothy waves,
And scrambling to the shore.

The Walrus and the Carpenter
Walked on a mile or so,
And then they rested on a rock
Conveniently low:
And all the little Oysters stood
And waited in a row.

'The time has come,' the Walrus said,
'To talk of many things:
Of shoes – and ships – and sealing wax –
Of cabbages – and kings –
And why the sea is boiling hot –
And whether pigs have wings.'

'But wait a bit,' the Oysters cried,
  'Before we have our chat;
For some of us are out of breath,
  And all of us are fat!'
'No hurry!' said the Carpenter.
  They thanked him much for that.

'A loaf of bread,' the Walrus said,
  'Is what we chiefly need:
Pepper and vinegar besides
  Are very good indeed –
Now if you're ready, Oysters dear,
  We can begin to feed.'

'But not on us!' the Oysters cried,
Turning a little blue.
'After such kindness, that would be
A dismal thing to do!'
'The night is fine,' the Walrus said.
'Do you admire the view?'

'It was so kind of you to come!
And you are very nice!'
The Carpenter said nothing but
'Cut us another slice:
I wish you were not quite so deaf –
I've had to ask you twice!'

'It seems a shame,' the Walrus said,
'To play them such a trick,
After we've brought them out so far,
And made them trot so quick!'
The Carpenter said nothing but
'The butter's spread too thick!'

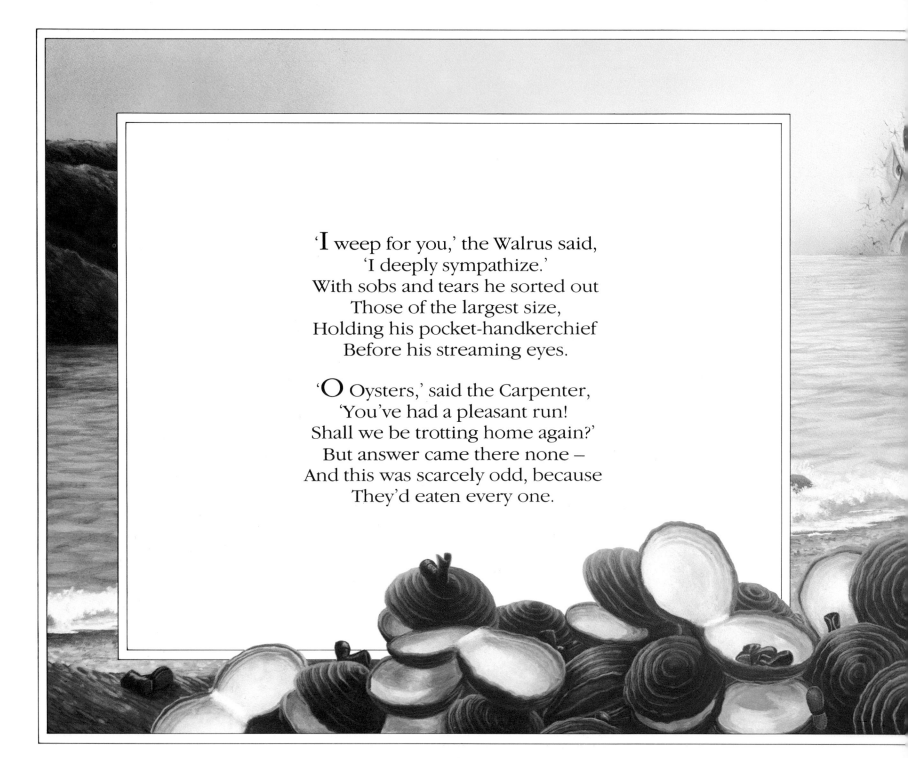

'I weep for you,' the Walrus said,
'I deeply sympathize.'
With sobs and tears he sorted out
Those of the largest size,
Holding his pocket-handkerchief
Before his streaming eyes.

'O Oysters,' said the Carpenter,
'You've had a pleasant run!
Shall we be trotting home again?'
But answer came there none –
And this was scarcely odd, because
They'd eaten every one.

# —·A-SITTING ON A GATE·—

I'll tell thee everything I can;
There's little to relate.
I saw an aged aged man,
A-sitting on a gate.
'Who are you, aged man?' I said.
'And how is it you live?'
And his answer trickled through my head
Like water through a sieve.

He said, 'I look for butterflies
That sleep among the wheat:
I make them into mutton-pies,
And sell them in the street.
I sell them unto men,' he said,
'Who sail on stormy seas;
And that's the way I get my bread –
A trifle, if you please.'

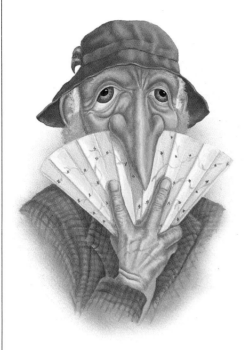

But I was thinking of a plan
To dye one's whiskers green,
And always use so large a fan
That they could not be seen.
So, having no reply to give
To what the old man said,
I cried, 'Come, tell me how you live!'
And thumped him on the head.

His accents mild took up the tale:
He said 'I go my ways,
And when I find a mountain-rill,
I set it in a blaze;
And thence they make a stuff they call
Rowland's Macassar Oil –
Yet twopence-halfpenny is all
They give me for my toil.'

But I was thinking of a way
To feed oneself on batter,
And so go on from day to day
Getting a little fatter.
I shook him well from side to side,
Until his face was blue:
'Come, tell me how you live,' I cried,
'And what it is you do!'

He said, 'I hunt for haddocks' eyes
Among the heather bright,
And work them into waistcoat-buttons
In the silent night.
And these I do not sell for gold
Or coin of silvery shine,
But for a copper halfpenny,
And that will purchase nine.

'I sometimes dig for buttered rolls,
Or set limed twigs for crabs;
I sometimes search the grassy knolls
For wheels of Hansom-cabs.
And that's the way' (he gave a wink)
'By which I get my wealth –
And very gladly will I drink
Your Honour's noble health.'

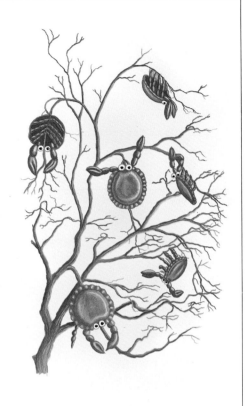

I heard him then, for I had just
Completed my design
To keep the Menai bridge from rust
By boiling it in wine.
I thanked him much for telling me
The way he got his wealth,
But chiefly for his wish that he
Might drink my noble health.

And now, if e'er by chance I put
My fingers into glue,
Or madly squeeze a right-hand foot
Into a left-hand shoe.
Or if I drop upon my toe
A very heavy weight,
I weep, for it reminds me so,
Of that old man I used to know —

Whose look was mild, whose speech was slow,
Whose hair was whiter than the snow,
Whose face was very like a crow,
With eyes, like cinders, all aglow,
Who seemed distracted with his woe,
Who rocked his body to and fro,
And muttered mumblingly and low,
As if his mouth were full of dough,
Who snorted like a buffalo —
That summer evening long ago,
A-sitting on a gate.

# HOW DOTH
## —·— THE ·—
# LITTLE CROCODILE

How doth the little crocodile
Improve his shining tail,
And pour the waters of the Nile
On every golden scale!

How cheerfully he seems to grin,
How neatly spreads his claws,
And welcomes little fishes in
With gently smiling jaws!

# YOU ARE
## — · OLD , · —
# FATHER WILLIAM

'You are old, Father William,' the young man said,
'And your hair has become very white;
And yet you incessantly stand on your head –
Do you think, at your age, it is right?'

'In my youth,' Father William replied to his son,
'I feared it might injure the brain;
But, now that I'm perfectly sure I have none,
Why, I do it again and again.'

'You are old,' said the youth, 'as I mentioned before,
    And have grown most uncommonly fat;
Yet you turned a back-somersault in at the door –
    Pray, what is the reason of that?'

'In my youth,' said the sage, as he shook his grey locks,
    'I kept all my limbs very supple
By the use of this ointment – one shilling the box –
    Allow me to sell you a couple?'

'You are old,' said the youth, 'and your jaws are too weak
For anything tougher than suet;
Yet you finished the goose, with the bones and the beak –
Pray, how did you manage to do it?'

'In my youth,' said his father, 'I took to the law,
And argued each case with my wife;
And the muscular strength, which it gave to my jaw,
Has lasted the rest of my life.'

'You are old,' said the youth, 'one would hardly suppose
That your eye was as steady as ever;
Yet you balanced an eel on the end of your nose –
What made you so awfully clever?'

'I have answered three questions, and that is enough,'
Said his father; 'don't give yourself airs!
Do you think I can listen all day to such stuff?
Be off, or I'll kick you down stairs!'

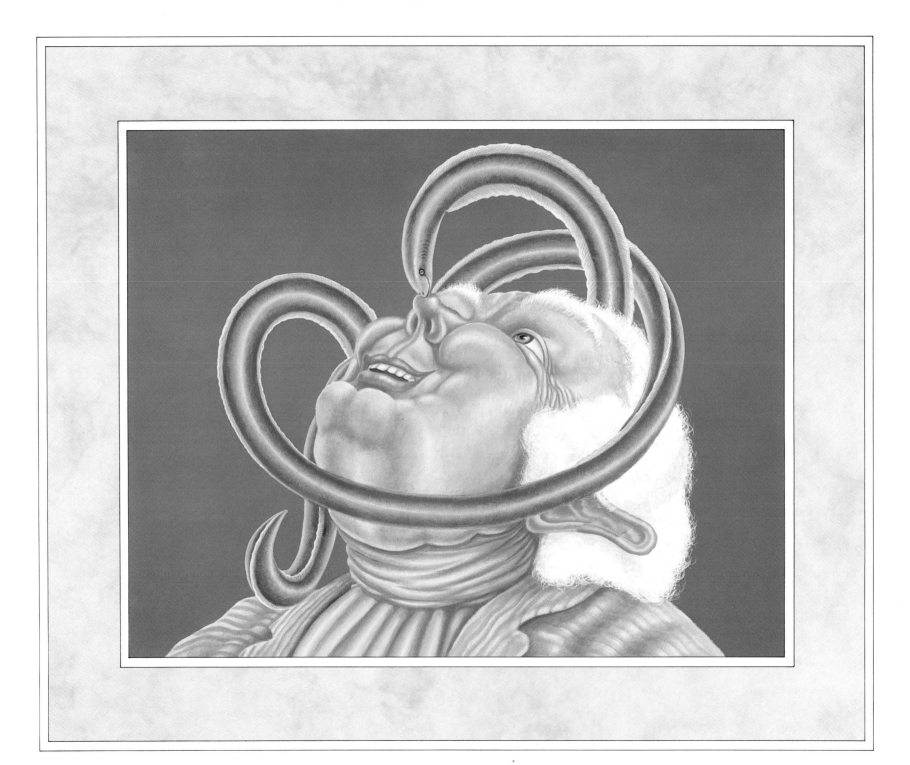

# — · THE LOBSTER QUADRILLE · —

'Will you walk a little faster?' said a whiting to a snail.
'There's a porpoise close behind us, and he's treading on my tail.
See how eagerly the lobsters and the turtles all advance!
They are waiting on the shingle – will you come and join the dance?
Will you, won't you, will you, won't you, will you join the dance?
Will you, won't you, will you, won't you, won't you join the dance?

'You can really have no notion how delightful it will be,
When they take us up and throw us, with the lobsters, out to sea!'
But the snail replied, 'Too far, too far!' and gave a look askance –
Said he thanked the whiting kindly, but he would not join the dance.
Would not, could not, would not, could not, would not join the dance.
Would not, could not, would not, could not, could not join the dance.

'What matters it how far we go?' his scaly friend replied.
'There is another shore, you know, upon the other side.
The further off from England the nearer is to France –
Then turn not pale, beloved snail, but come and join the dance.
Will you, won't you, will you, won't you, will you join the dance?
Will you, won't you, will you, won't you, won't you join the dance?'

# · THE ·
# GARDENER'S SONG

He thought he saw an Elephant,
That practised on a fife:
He looked again, and found it was
A letter from his wife.
'At length I realise', he said,
'The bitterness of Life!'

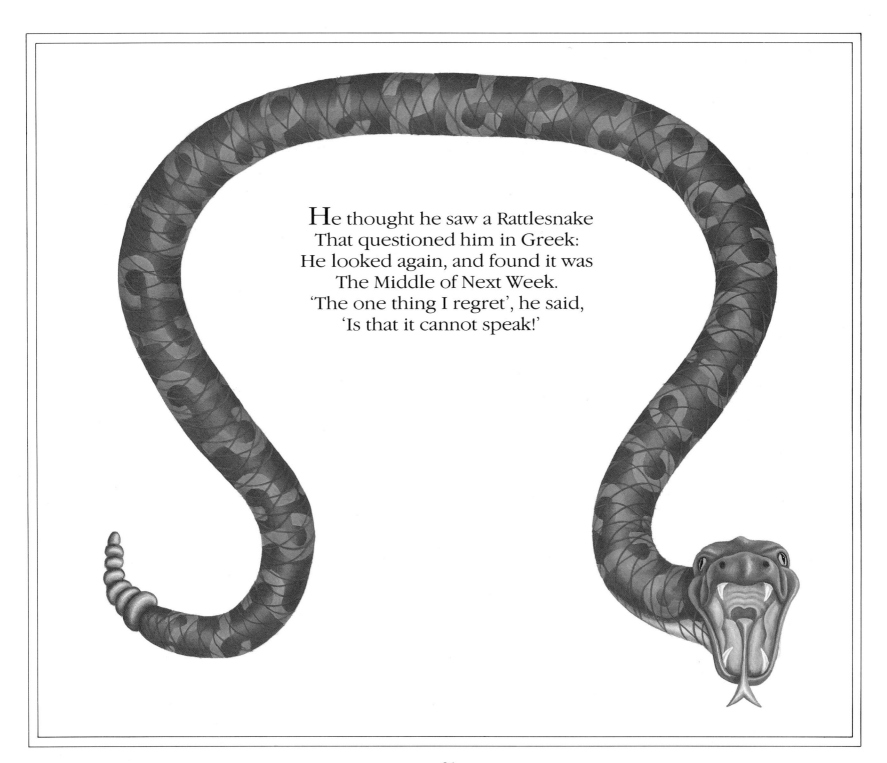

He thought he saw a Rattlesnake
That questioned him in Greek:
He looked again, and found it was
The Middle of Next Week.
'The one thing I regret', he said,
'Is that it cannot speak!'

He thought he saw a Buffalo
Upon the chimney-piece:
He looked again, and found it was
His Sister's Husband's Niece.
'Unless you leave this house', he said,
'I'll send for the Police!'

He thought he saw a Banker's Clerk
Descending from the bus:
He looked again, and found it was
A Hippopotamus:
'If this should stay to dine', he said,
'There won't be much for us!'

He thought he saw a Kangaroo
That worked a coffee-mill:
He looked again, and found it was
A Vegetable-Pill.
'Were I to swallow this', he said,
'I should be very ill!'

He thought he saw a Coach-and-Four
That stood beside his bed:
He looked again, and found it was
A Bear without a Head.
'Poor thing', he said, 'poor silly thing!
It's waiting to be fed!'

He thought he saw an Albatross
That fluttered round the lamp:
He looked again, and found it was
A Penny-Postage-Stamp.
'You'd best be getting home', he said:
'The nights are very damp!'

He thought he saw a Garden-Door
That opened with a key:
He looked again, and found it was
A Double Rule of Three:
'And all its mystery', he said,
'Is clear as day to me!'

# · TURTLE SOUP ·

Beautiful Soup, so rich and green,
Waiting in a hot tureen!
Who for such dainties would not stoop?
Soup of the evening, beautiful Soup!
Soup of the evening, beautiful Soup!
Beau—ootiful Soo—oop!
Beau—ootiful Soo—oop!
Soo—oop of the e—e—evening,
Beautiful, beautiful Soup!

Beautiful Soup! Who cares for fish,
Game, or any other dish!
Who would not give all else for two p
ennyworth only of beautiful Soup?
Pennyworth only of beautiful Soup?
Beau—ootiful Soo—oop!
Beau—ootiful Soo—oop!
Soo—oop of the e—e—evening,
Beautiful, beauti—FUL SOUP!

# — · JABBERWOCKY · —

'Twas brillig, and the slithy toves
Did gyre and gimble in the wabe;
All mimsy were the borogoves,
And the mome raths outgrabe.

"Beware the Jabberwock, my son!
The jaws that bite, the claws that catch!
Beware the Jubjub bird, and shun
The frumious Bandersnatch!"

He took his vorpal sword in hand:
Long time the manxome foe he sought –
So rested he by the Tumtum tree,
And stood awhile in thought.

And as in uffish thought he stood,
The Jabberwock, with eyes of flame,
Came whiffling through the tulgey wood,
And burbled as it came!

One, two! One, two! And through and through
The vorpal blade went snicker-snack!
He left it dead, and with its head
He went galumphing back.

"And hast thou slain the Jabberwock?
Come to my arms, my beamish boy!
O frabjous day! Callooh! Callay!"
He chortled in his joy.

'Twas brillig, and the slithy toves
Did gyre and gimble in the wabe;
All mimsy were the borogoves,
And the mome raths outgrabe.